READING CORNER

Pablo the Painter

A humorous
story

First published in 2006 by
Franklin Watts
338 Euston Road
London
NW1 3BH

Franklin Watts Australia
Hachette Children's Books
Level 17/207 Kent Street
Sydney
NSW 2000

A CIP catalogue record for this book is available
from the British Library.

ISBN 0 7496 6559 9 (hbk)
ISBN 0 7496 6571 8 (pbk)

Series Editor: Jackie Hamley
Series Advisors: Dr Barrie Wade, Dr Hilary Minns
Series Design: Peter Scoulding

The author and publisher would like to thank Robert Kearney
for permission to use the photograph on page 4 (top).

Printed in China

Pablo the Painter

Written by
Mick Gowar

Illustrated by
Fabiano Fiorin

FRANKLIN WATTS
LONDON • SYDNEY

Mick Gowar

"I teach at an art school in Cambridge. One day, a pigeon flew in through the window, but he wasn't a brilliant painter like Pierre!"

Fabiano Fiorin

"I live in Venice in Italy. I've been painting since I was in nappies. I love it because it always puts me in a good mood. I also have a pigeon friend. His name is Columbus."

Pablo was a painter.

He lived in a tiny flat in Paris.

Pablo was a wonderful painter.

He could paint anything ...

people on horseback ...

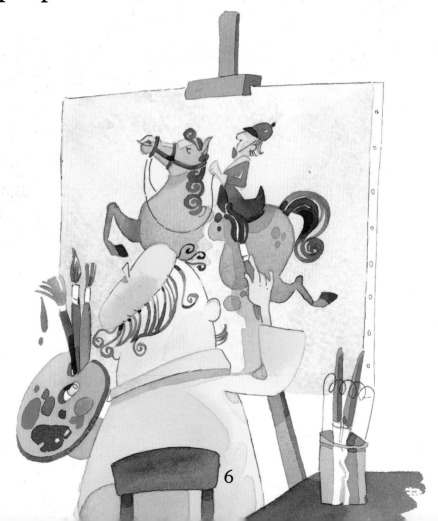

boats on the sea ...

puppies and kittens.

Pablo liked painting food best of all.

He painted potatoes

and pineapples ...

peaches and
poppadoms ...

pears and plum pudding.

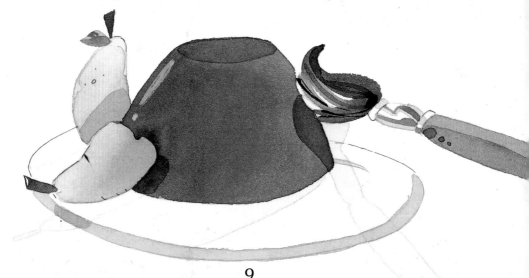

Pablo painted food because he could not afford to buy tasty things to eat. No one ever bought his paintings.

All Pablo could afford was bread.
He ate bread and jam for breakfast,
bread pudding for lunch and bread
and cheese for supper.

When Pablo finished eating, he scattered the breadcrumbs on his balcony for Pierre the pigeon who lived on the roof.

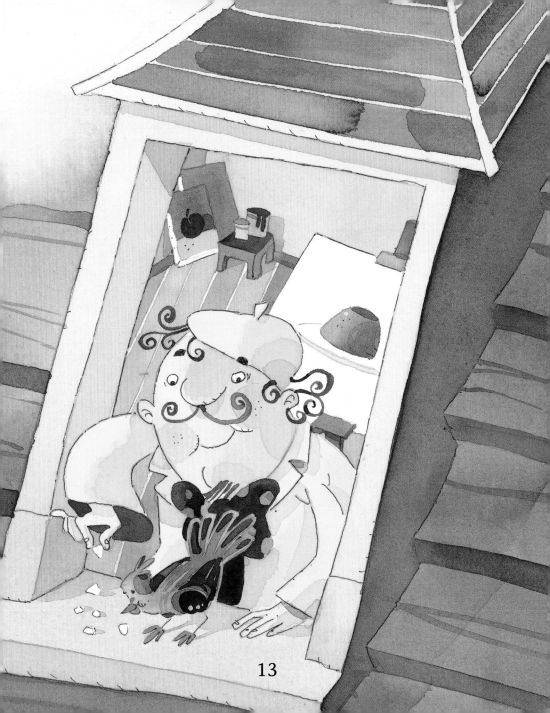

13

Not more than a pigeon's flight away
was the grandest house in Paris.

It was the palace where the
President of France lived.

The President was not happy.
"This place is too dark and gloomy,"
he complained. "It's full of pictures
of soldiers and shipwrecks.

"I want some new pictures, with bright colours – pictures of delicious things to eat, such as pineapples, pears and peaches."

"I know the very painter!"
replied Gaston, his secretary.
"He lives near here."

18

"We will go and see his paintings
this afternoon," said the President.
"Go, Gaston! Tell him to be ready!"

19

Pablo was very excited. "The President is coming to see my paintings!" he told Pierre.

"I've got one painting to finish," he said. "My masterpiece! And I only have ten minutes before the President arrives!"

Pierre perched on the balcony rail. "Coo!" he cooed, but Pablo was too busy painting to give him more crumbs.

"Cooo!" Pierre fluttered into Pablo's flat. There sat the biggest, most golden, most delicious loaf of bread Pierre had ever seen.

"Coooo!" Pierre flew towards the bread to take a few crumbs, when ...

CRASH!

"Oh, no!" cried Pablo. "Look what you've done! All my paintings – ruined!"

KNOCK! KNOCK!

"Who's there?" asked Pablo.

"The President!" said Gaston, and

he and the President marched in.

The President frowned and pointed.
"Are those ... are those your
paintings?" he gasped. Pablo nodded.
He was too upset to speak.

"Why, they're ... they're ..." stuttered
the President. "The colours! The
shapes! They're ... wonderful!

"They're ... fantastic! *Magnifique!* I'll buy them all to hang in the palace! Gaston, pay him lots of money!"

"I like your parrot," said the President.

"Coo!" said Pierre.

"That's odd," said the President,

"he sounds just like a pigeon."

"He isn't a parrot or a pigeon," said Pablo. "He's a painter bird – the only one!"

Notes for parents and teachers

READING CORNER has been structured to provide maximum support for new readers. The stories may be used by adults for sharing with young children. Primarily, however, the stories are designed for newly independent readers, whether they are reading these books in bed at night, or in the reading corner at school or in the library.

Starting to read alone can be a daunting prospect. READING CORNER helps by providing visual support and repeating words and phrases, while making reading enjoyable. These books will develop confidence in the new reader, and encourage a love of reading that will last a lifetime!

If you are reading this book with a child, here are a few tips:

1. Make reading fun! Choose a time to read when you and the child are relaxed and have time to share the story.

2. Encourage children to reread the story, and to retell the story in their own words, using the illustrations to remind them what has happened.

3. Give praise! Remember that small mistakes need not always be corrected.

READING CORNER covers three grades of early reading ability, with three levels at each grade. Each level has a certain number of words per story, indicated by the number of bars on the spine of the book, to allow you to choose the right book for a young reader:

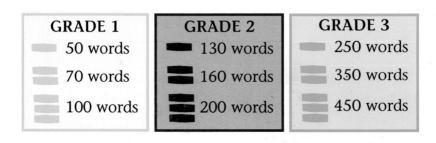

GRADE 1	GRADE 2	GRADE 3
50 words	130 words	250 words
70 words	160 words	350 words
100 words	200 words	450 words